sland

Northern Forest

Woodland
House

East
Mountains

← fairy path   river →

ountains

Beach
Cottage

bridge →

path to
beach

Japanese
House

S0-AWQ-858

fairy island

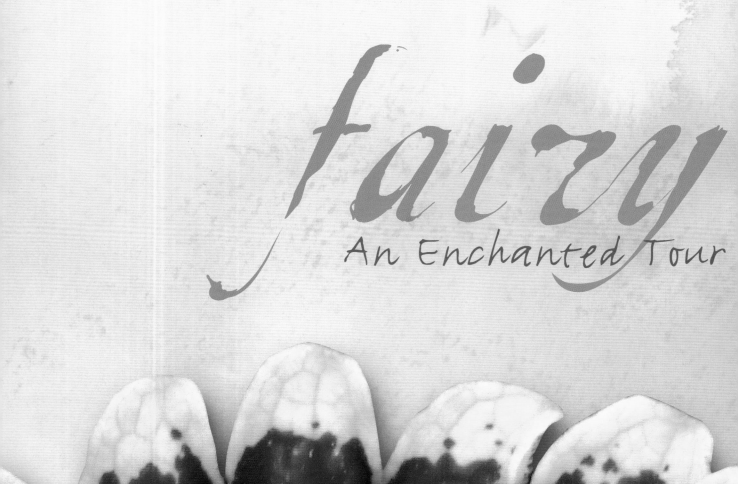

fairy
An Enchanted Tour

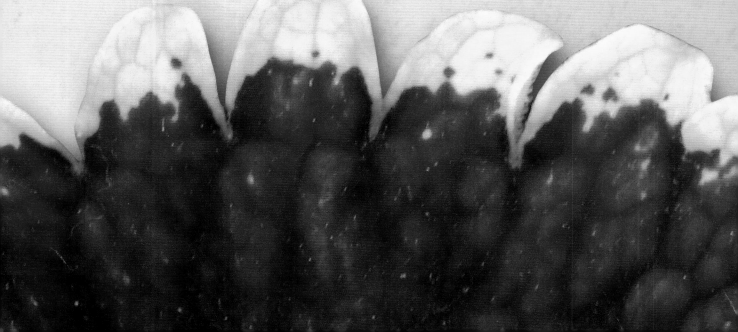

island
of the Homes of the Little Folk

Discovered and documented by Christine Newkirk

Created by Laura C. Martin and Cameron Martin

BLACK DOG
& LEVENTHAL
PUBLISHERS
NEW YORK

To Jack and Michael, who always let us believe!

Copyright © 2005 by Laura Martin

All rights reserved. No part of this book may be reproduced in any form or
by any electronic or mechanical means including information storage and
retrieval systems without the written permission of the publisher.

ISBN: 1-579912-455-0

Designed by Liz Driesbach

Manufactured in Thailand

Published by Black Dog & Leventhal Publishers, Inc.
151 West 19th Street New York, New York 10011

Distributed by Workman Publishing Company
708 Broadway New York, New York 10003

g f e d c b a

Library of Congress Cataloging-in-Publication
Data available on file.

contents

Dear Reader,

My grandmother, Christine Newkirk, was a remarkable woman. A botanist by training, she lived on a small, remote island for most of her life, studying and drawing orchids indigenous to the region. During the last few years of her life, however, she made a discovery that changed her life — and mine. She found tiny, perfect houses that she felt could only have been built by fairies. Although she wanted me to come to see this miraculously small world myself, due to the distance and isolation of the island and my parent's reluctance to send me, I was never allowed to visit her.

So, my grandmother did the next best thing. She carefully documented, in journal entries, photographs and drawings, all that she found. At her death, she left me everything she owned, including her home on the island. But it is this, the scrapbook about the fairies, that I hold most dear. She has made the fairy world seem so real to me that it seems as if I could simply close my eyes and see the fairies themselves.

The book is too much of a treasure to keep to myself and so I share it with you. I hope that you, too, will enter the world of the fairies and be captured by their magic.

Katherine Newkirk

Dear Katherine,

You will never guess what I found yesterday, walking through the woods looking for orchids — a tiny house that must belong to fairies! As a botanist, I am used to looking for plants close to the ground, otherwise I don't think I would have noticed it. But when I bent to take a closer look — what a beautiful sight met my eyes!

There stood a perfectly tiny house covered with pine bark, with a roof of soft, green moss. A door made of gray lichen stood slightly open

Dogwood (Cornus florida)

and I stood still for a long time, waiting to see if a fairy would come out, but no one ever did. Finally, I crept away quietly, promising myself to come back another day.

I know that there are those who will think that I am crazy, for no one has ever actually seen a fairy. And, of course, I have no proof that this really is a fairy house. But, it is so beautiful and exquisite, I cannot imagine who else could have built it.

Love, Grandmother

the
woodland
cabin

I returned to the house today with my camera and sketch book, terribly afraid that I had dreamed the whole thing. I wasn't even sure I could find it again, but moving as quietly as I could, I slowly crept through the underbrush until I caught sight of the small wheelbarrow in the front yard.

The house was as exquisite as I had remembered. The soft moss of the roof seemed untouched by the storms we have had in the past few weeks. It camouflages the house perfectly. The lichen-covered door stood slightly open, and I remained quite still for a very long time, hoping that one of the tiny occupants would come out — or in. Even though I sat almost motionless for nearly an hour, I never caught sight of anything that looked like a fairy.

Wheelbarrow — ingenious construction, sides are pine bark. Handles made from curved branches of poplar.

silver poplar (Populus alba)

Beautiful lichen-covered twigs used to make chair.

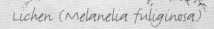
Lichen (Melanelia fuliginosa)

Fishing pole — made from purplish twigs of dogwood saplings.

The line is a thin piece of vine — hooked at the end. Bait could be inchworms. . .

Moss handle

Dogwood (Cornus florida)

The basket must be for their catch. Maybe just-hatched tadpoles?

Lichen (Daedalea contragosa)

1/2"

Wheel — I think — was carved from a piece of hard lichen.

14

Katherine,
It has been raining
without stop for several
days now. I am eager to
get out of the house and
resume my walks on the
island and, of course, to
go back to the fairy
house. In the meantime,
I sit and look at the
photographs I made during
my last visit there and
draw and think about
you and wonder how you
are doing.

Back of the house – like the other sides –
is covered with pine bark. Caulking is a
combination of moss and lichen. Entire house
measures 24 inches deep, 22 inches across,
about the size of an old-fashioned ice-box.

Back door is split – top half opens separately
from bottom. I can just imagine a little
fairy child at the door, waving goodbye
to her father.

shrubs are tiny Santolina –
only about 4 inches tall.

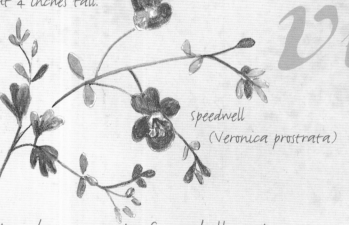

speedwell
(Veronica prostrata)

Window boxes made from hollowed
branches, filled with soil and planted
with speedwell. They match the violas
(Viola cornuta) in the front garden.

The chimney is remarkably sturdy. The red rocks (more like gravel really) are caulked with lichen (Ramalina stenospora).

May 5
I saw the inside of the house today! The interior is, if possible, even more beautiful than the outside. Each piece of furniture is a work of art. Each tiny accessory seems to have been made with loving care.

Asparagus fern around shelves (Asparagus setaceus) and a sprig of lavender is lying on the shelf probably to scent the room

4"

21

The dining table is in front of a big, open bay window. I must have just missed them today. Their lunch – a single strawberry – was still on the table

Pansy (viola)

Pansy petal stuffed with milkweed makes a pillow.

The rocking chair back is one cap of dried turkey tail fungus (Trametes versicolor). They also use it for display shelves – must be strong.

pansy

I never thought about music being part of fairy life until I saw this banjo and music stand. The music is written on paper birch bark. I can't read it – wonder if they simply play the music of the wood.

Hickory (Carya cordiformis)

Purple pitcher plant (sarracenia purpurea)

Don't know whether piece of the mantle is a mirror – or art. Made from pitcher plant, framed with curved twigs.

The banjo is made from a split hickory nut. strets are reeds of some sort – strings are strands of grass.

1/2"

Eastern
white pine
(Pinus strobes)

5"

Paper birch
(Betula papyrifera)

birchbark

Exquisite lampshade made from the tip of
eastern white pine cone. I did not know they
grew on the island, will have to look for them.
Slender chain and pull for lamp made from
pink amaranth plant (Amaranthus caudatus).

25

The acorn cup and bowl only seem big enough for tiny morsels.
The chest is covered with more of that beautiful lichen, and its handles
are seed pods of rattlesnake plantain (Goodyera pubescens).

. Pillows are coleus leaves. Bedspread is ginkgo leaves sewn together. I must look for sewing tools and thread. What could they use for a needle?

Coleus
(Coleus blumei)

Ginkgo
(Ginkgo biloba)

Grass rug —
Calamagrostis
acutifolia

Bittersweet grows all over the island. The fairies left a piece on the chest by the breakfast tray. I wonder if they have found a medicinal use for it? I've never heard of one. I must write Dr. Gray at Cambridge and ask him.

Bittersweet
(Celastrus
scandens)

29

poppy

Window shutters
from monkey puzzle tree,
araucaria. Flower vase –
tip of chili pepper.

Monkey puzzle
(Aracuaria)

Poppy
(Paparer rhoeas)

2"

Lampshade from a poppy seed head.
Excellent choice, as it is thick enough
to be sturdy but translucent
enough to allow light through.

small bedside table made from flat piece of bark,
base is curly twigs, secured with moss.

Boots! Out of peanuts.
I wonder how long they last?
I suspect fairies step very lightly,
though. Spurs seem to be made
out of tips of cedar cones.

Peanut (Vigna
unguiculata)

peanut

Wardrobe covered with palm frond, edged
with moss, and latched with a poplar twig.

Dear Katherine,

This morning I went to get fresh eggs at the Barnes' farm.
As always, Mrs. Barnes was full of stories.
"Someone's been stealing my smallest
fruits and vegetables," she said,
and suddenly I was very interested.

"What's happened to them?"
I asked. She smiled as she pulled out
a tiny, perfect bouquet.

"I don't know," she whispered,
"but whenever something is gone, I find
a wee gift like this in its place."

Bouquet flowers: mustard blossoms
(Brassica oleracea), rockcress (Arabis alpina),
blue phlox (Phlox divaricata)

When I returned, Mrs. Barnes was not home, so,
feeling only a little guilty, I walked straight to the

finally I saw, nestled next to a corn plant, a tiny bouquet, identical to the one I had seen yesterday. I examined the ground and soon found a narrow path leading through the corn. I followed it (walking carefully!) until it ended, at another fairy house!

Love, Grandmother

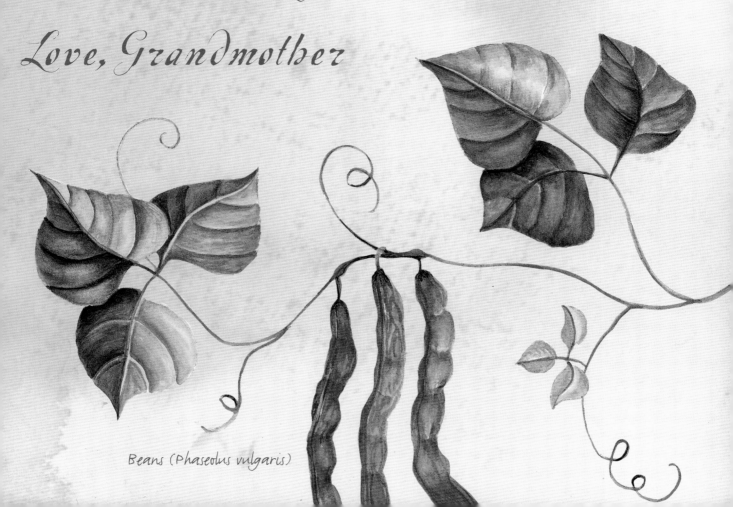

Beans (Phaseolus vulgaris)

the farm
house

July 3

The outside of the house seems to be made from a smooth, light-colored mud, supported with cinnamon stick beams. The roof is made of straw and split cinnamon sticks were cut to make window boxes. Window frames are made from tiny cut reeds. The grass outside the house is almost as tall as the cinnamon stick rail fence! A graceful arbor, covered with tiny rockcress blossoms (Arabis alpina) arches over the kitchen window. Bright blue blossoms of lobelia (Lobelia erinus) brighten the corners while creeping phlox (Phlox subulata) softens the edges of the fence. Tools and the bee kelp indicate that this is a thriving farm.

Windowbox flowers
(Latin name)

Arbor — rockcress blossoms
(Arabis alpina)

This is obviously a working farm for the fairies. A pitch fork, rake and shovel lean against the fence.

tulip

4"

Tulip poplar tree
(Liriodendron tulipifera)

A tiny scarecrow indicates that even fairies have pests. Hat made from blossom of tulip poplar tree (Liriodendron tulipifera). What could such a little scarecrow scare away? Mosquitoes?

39

←

Very small vegetables peek out from the black earth. Looking like miniscule cabbages, brussell sprouts grow alongside white pearl onions. In the next row, red radishes poke above ground. Beyond this, miniature corn plants are lined up in a neat row. I suspect the fairies bring water from the well to put on their plants. They obviously work hard on the garden — not a weed to be seen. Scarecrow must be doing a good job too — everything looks perfectly healthy.

These fairies are so small that they need a ladder to harvest the tomatoes.

The wheelbarrow only fits two cherry tomatoes at a time.

Cherry tomatoes (Lycopersicon lycopersicum)

What a discovery!
I'd always wondered
where that
miniature corn
on the cob came
from, now I know!
Fairy farms.

Corn (Zea mays rugosa)

A beehive indicates they raise bees, but
what could be small enough to fit inside?
Wonder if there is a species of very small
bees? Those big golden northern bumble bees
would be the size of sheep for fairies. Even
honey bees are over 1/2 inch long. Must
ask my entomologist friend, Dr. Chisler.

A well house at the edge of the vegetable garden is topped with a weather vane. The ends of the arrows are each tipped with a different type of flower – wonder if they use colors to indicate compass directions?

Finally saw inside today. Kitchen seems to be the main room of the house and it is wonderful! Wish I had such a kitchen to work in. The counter tops are made from cinnamon sticks split in half and the cabinets are bay leaves. The back splash is a variety of beans and peas. Curtains at the window are leaves from the flowering cabbage plant (Brassica oleracea).

Blueberries
(Vaccinium ashei)

47

A basket on the floor holds a variety of peppers. Miniature gourds hanging over sink are probably used for various purposes.

string beans
(Phaseolus vulgaris)

The sink is a turned wooden bowl — looks like cherry wood — with a fiddlehead fern for a faucet. Around the sink is eggshell mosaic.

49

Herbs hang down from the shelves,
tied in small bundles.

Overlapping bay leaves with
lady-pea knobs make perfect
cabinet doors. The veins in the
leaves make a simple — but
stunning — pattern. The colors
are so rich and earthy.
→

3"

Tea cups made from
chili peppers (Capsicum annuum)!

Oven is obviously a dried acorn squash on a mushroom cap with
an okra pod stove pipe. It must smell wonderful when it is hot.
Table is a slice of acorn squash on a piece of ginger root.

cinnamon

Bell pepper
(Capsicum annuum)

seems that the
stove is stoked with
cinnamon sticks,
as pepper baskets
full of them
are close by.

Rolling pin is
a twig with
two handles
carved into
the ends.

The most beautiful piece in the house is a 5 inch square quilt hanging on the wall. It is made of 17 different spices and seeds.

FIRST ROW: fennel seeds, chili pepper flakes, paprika, ground ginger

SECOND ROW: ground red pepper, celery seeds, black peppercorns, mung beans

THIRD ROW: French lentils, mustard seeds, red lentils, sesame seeds

FOURTH ROW: ground cinnamon, cornmeal, ground cloves, ground mustard seeds

All against a background of poppy seeds

High chair seat is made from small cattails. Back and tray are dried artichoke petals. Teddy Bear itself? Eyes are definitely black peppercorns, the body seems to be the fuzz from the inside of a cattail.

For a moment, I thought I was finally looking at a fairy! It took a moment to realize that I was only seeing a toy teddy bear sitting in the high chair. A broken gingerbread man cookie makes me think that the fairies have just left. How could I miss them again!

1"

57

quince

It looks as if someone just took off these green pepper boots with corn shuck laces. I suppose the shiny peppers are waterproof and make good footwear for the fairies.

Cantaloupe
(Cucumis melo)

Quince
(Chaenomeles quinoa)

Window shutters on walls and door are bright slices of dried quince. The door itself is made from cantaloupe rind! It looks sturdy — thick, almost like leather.

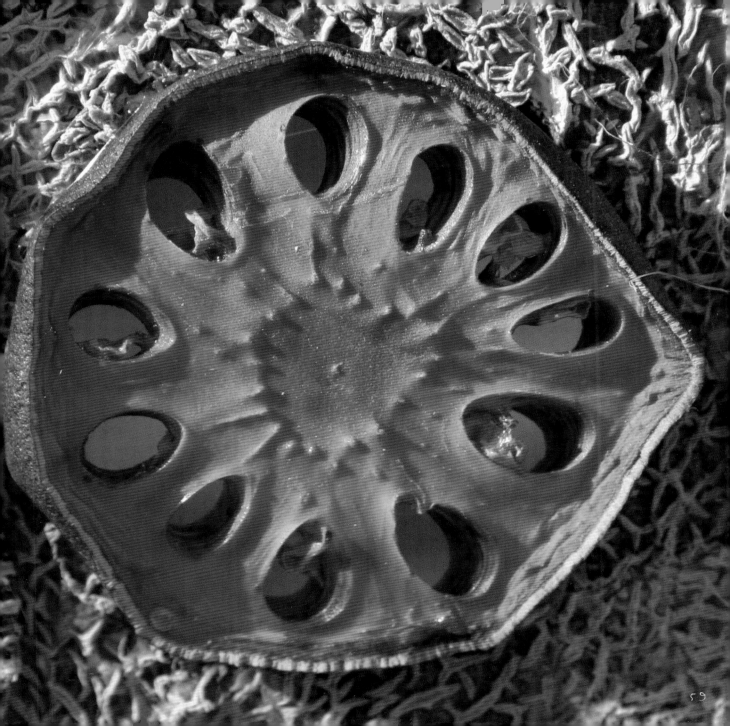

Dear Katherine,   June 12

I was on the windward side of the island today, following the tracks of a bristle-thighed curlew when I saw prints like I'd never seen before — less than an inch long, with five perfect toe marks. I could not identify them as bird tracks but then it occurred to me, maybe they were made by a fairy! Perhaps there is another fairy house on the island. I know about the menehunes, the elfin-like creatures

Pink orchid (Dendrobium)

that were supposedly stone workers long before humans came to this island. Could they still be here?

I followed the footsteps to a stretch of protected beach, and there it was! The most enticing cottage you can imagine. Made of bamboo and shells with an open porch, it was amazingly inviting.

I crouched behind an acacia shrub for a long time, waiting to see some sign of activity, but I never saw anyone. Legend says that the menehunes only work at night, perhaps these fairies do the same.

While I sat watching the house, I noticed that it was constructed from materials that they could find within a stone's throw of where I was sitting. When I bent down, with my face close to the sandy beach, I could see through the open porch and noticed that they had used a spray of orchids as a room divider.

Love, Grandmother

the beach cottage

June 13

Could not stay away. House appeared even more enticing today. I crept
closer to take some measurements and found that the house is about
15 inches tall, about 22 inches wide.

The solid walls are made from sand, shells and mud, mixed together
to make a tabby. Back screen is woven bamboo, which seems to be the
structural material of choice. Many different kinds grow on island.
Support beams and foundation poles made from Bambusa indigena.

It is in an amazing spot, right at the edge of the beach, protected
by some low-growing shrubs. Small flowers (Pentas lanceolata, I think)
are planted outside the doors, making it all the more beautiful.

The swing is made out of a
combination of bamboo poles and
coconut fibers. Poles are attached to
a cross piece with raffia ties.

Palm used for a variety of purposes, individual leaf fronds, pulled off mid-rib and used for roof.

sea heather (Erica carnea) planted around the house.

Palm tree
(Phoenix canariensis)

palmtree

65

stunning setting!
Front of house
faces the ocean, the
back is toward the
mountains, great
view wherever you look.

Bamboo (Bambusa indigena)

3"

Telescope made from
graduated sizes of bamboo.
Can't tell what they
used for optics.

↑ seems that there is an interest in science, at least astronomy.
Map of constellation, Orion, paper made from pounded mulberry leaves.
And the star markings must be inked with mulberry juice.

69

Illicium verum
star anise. Fruit
is used for curtain
tie backs. This tree
is native to China,
never seen it growing
on island. Wonder how
the fairies obtained
the fruit?

star anise
(Illicium verum)

moss

A lurid
dwarf triton
makes a
perfect planter.
It is filled with
Pentas.

1"

→

spanish moss
(Tillandsia
usneoides) seems
to be an insulation
material.

Dwarf triton

Obviously children live in this house. I saw the coziest crib imaginable, and the rocking horse is – naturally – made from a sea horse. The prickly spine is covered with a shell and fiber saddle.

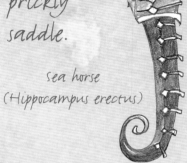

sea horse
(Hippocampus erectus)

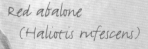

Red abalone
(Haliotis rufescens)

They must love to play games. Checker board is an inch square. Pieces are not much bigger than grains of sand. Chairs made from red abalone with fairy tern-feather cushions.

Mattresses made from feathers from the white tern. My reading indicates that this bird is sometimes called fairy tern on the island. Now I understand where the name comes from... Headboard for the bed made from bay scallop, (Argopecten irradians).

White tern
(Gygis alba rothschildi)

5"

scallop (Argopecten irradians)

fairy tern

Hot tub is in the back of the house, adjacent to the dressing room with small steps right outside the door. No apparent means of heating the water, but these fairies are so sophisticated that I'm sure it is hot. I was reluctant to test the water myself as I didn't want to disturb anything.

sandals made from split bamboo.

77

The bikini is made from small white clam shells
(about 1/2 inch across) decorated with bits of red celosia.

The only enclosed
space is a dressing
room. Candles on
the wall are made
from wax poured
into small dwarf
triton shells.

triton

Bathrobe and towels are
woven from palm fibers.

3"

White abra clam
(Abra alba)

The mirror is
pink mica.

Both sink and tub are covered with a variety of small shells that look beautiful as well as giving structural strength.

The door to the outside is covered with tiny shells. The effect is so beautiful it took my breath away!

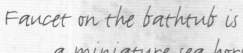

Faucet on the bathtub is a miniature sea horse (Hippocampus erectus).

shells

Beach bag made from ferns hammered into
mulberry leaves (Morus nigra). Wonder if ferns add strength
to the bag or are only for decoration?

These glasses are so small
I almost missed seeing them.
I can only imagine what a
tiny face they must fit.
The seat is made from sea glass
– polished smooth by the waves.

glass

Mulberry (morus nigra)

Bucket
and shovel.

Palm leaves used for flippers.
Must be waterproof - I'll have to
test this quality of the leaves.
Guess they enjoy swimming, and
they must be bold, for it seems as
if they would be swallowed by
even the tiniest fish!

sensitive plant is a weed on the island. Leaves close up when touched. Flowers are soft balls and must make perfect play balls for fairy children. They are soft, pretty and sweet scented.

sensitive plant
(schrankia microphylla)

Hibiscus
(Hibiscus rosa-sinensis)

I can't imagine anything more perfect than sitting in a palm-leaf beach chair underneath a hibiscus umbrella, watching the waves.

Dear Katherine,

Even here on the island, I am required (on occasion) to fulfill a social obligation. So, today I dusted off my finery and paid a call on the matriarch of the island, Mrs. Hugh Thompson. She was as charming as ever, asking about my research, then invited me to stroll through her garden. She declined to join me, however, as she felt some pain in her hip. I was delighted to escape into the sunshine and spent a pleasant hour walking through her formal garden. I had stopped to examine a particularly beautiful specimen of dahlia when I dropped my purse. As I bent to retrieve it, I saw what could only be described as a perfect formal garden complete with green hedges and potted flowers – in front of a beautiful gray stone house – all fairy size! I didn't even try to get closer but returned immediately to the house, my heart pounding in my chest.

I told Mrs. Thompson that I had seen an especially beautiful magnolia (Magnolia grandiflora) growing in the garden and requested permission to return and paint it. She graciously told me that I was welcome to return as often as I liked, but that she, regretfully, would be off island for the remainder of the summer. I was delighted! And hope to go back tomorrow.

Love, Grandmother

Magnolia grandiflora

the
garden
villa

August 2

What an exciting day it has been! This garden villa is the most
formal of any of the fairy houses I have seen thus far. The outside
walls are made of small gray stones, held in place with a mud mortar.
The roof appears to be layered hosta (Hosta plantaginea) leaves.
Tiny pots on either side of the door hold bright red miniature roses.
Exquisite pieces of gnarled wood are used for planters. A small pink
begonia just fits into a hollowed out knot. When I stood up and peeked
over the roof to see the back of the house, I was amazed at
how many different flowers were
growing in this small space.
It is all beautifully designed
and meticulously cared for.

2"

Tiny pots hold bright
red miniature roses
(Rosa "Baby Darling").

The vine growing on the house is Euonymus – I've always used it as a groundcover, but the rich, dark green leaves make perfect wall covering for the fairy house.

Asteromoea mongolica and
Abelia x grandiflora

Persian violets (Exacum affine)

93

95

Aug 5

A trademark fairy bouquet hangs in the dressing room, which obviously belongs to a lady. The dressing table top is pink larkspur, the skirt is made from red amaranth while the curtains at the window are from the green amaranth variety. The rug is a simple hosta leaf.

More shoes! They are made from the hard, dried bracts of thistle. Red yarrow blooms are used across the straps.

97

The mirror over the dressing table is a piece of pink mica —
shiny enough, I am sure, to reflect even the tiniest of faces.

Fairy bouquet of asparagus fern,
red yarrow, pink larkspur, lavender.

Red amaranth
(Amaranthus caudatus)

All kinds of vases and containers are found on the
dressing table, alongside the brush and comb (made from
the monkey puzzle pine). The sturdy tip that connects the
magnolia blossom to the branch was hollowed out to hold some
sort of lotion. Obviously, these are cosmetics, but the piece of
turquoise? I wonder if they grind it up to make eye shadow?

The coat made from white dove feathers is the most beautiful I've ever seen. The collar, cuffs and belt are made from velvety red cockscomb. Hanging on a door of lavender blossoms, it is exquisite.

4"

Cockscomb
(Celosia cristata)

cockscomb

→

Lampshade is a collage of tiny pieces of petals from spring flowers – pansy (Viola wittrockiana), viola (Viola cornuta), lobelia (Lobelia erinus), wall flower (Erysimum cheiri) and more. I wonder what they use for a light source. A candle? Couldn't be any bigger than a birthday candle.

The trim is pink amaranth.
It makes the lampshade look like a festive party hat.

lamb's ear

The divan looks incredibly soft
and inviting with its mattress
of cockscomb, its feather blanket
and pillows made from hosta
and lamb's ear leaves.

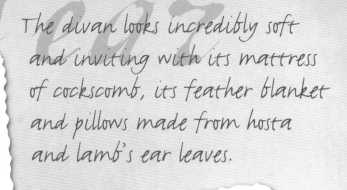

Cockscomb (Celosia cristata)

Lenten rose
(Helleborus niger)

Near the divan is a table made from a peacock feather
— the lampshade is a lenten rose blossom (Helleborus
niger). Gloves from the foxglove plant (Digitalis
purpurea), paper and a tiny pen sit on the table.

Globe amaranth (Gomphrena globosa)

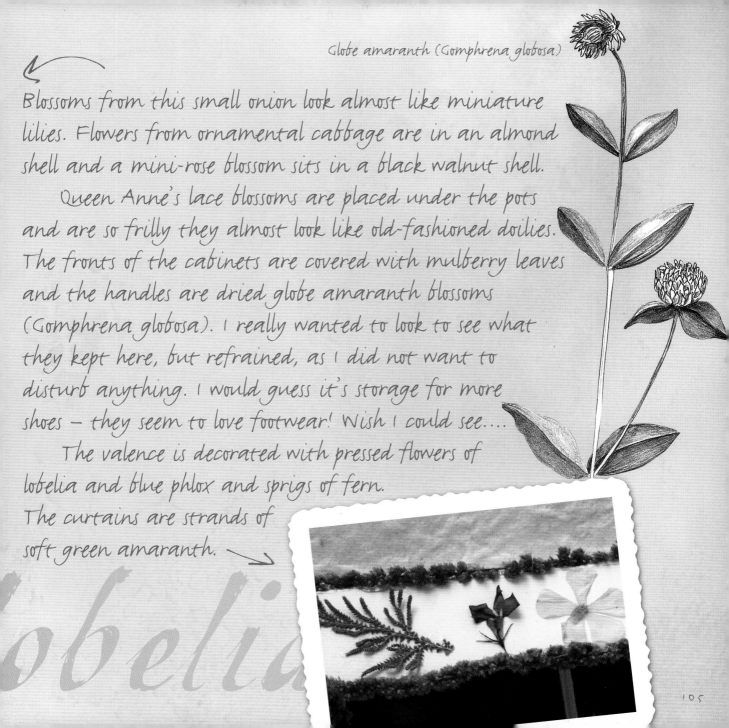

Blossoms from this small onion look almost like miniature lilies. Flowers from ornamental cabbage are in an almond shell and a mini-rose blossom sits in a black walnut shell.

Queen Anne's lace blossoms are placed under the pots and are so frilly they almost look like old-fashioned doilies. The fronts of the cabinets are covered with mulberry leaves and the handles are dried globe amaranth blossoms (Gomphrena globosa). I really wanted to look to see what they kept here, but refrained, as I did not want to disturb anything. I would guess it's storage for more shoes — they seem to love footwear! Wish I could see....

The valence is decorated with pressed flowers of lobelia and blue phlox and sprigs of fern. The curtains are strands of soft green amaranth.

The game room is a hand-some room and so masculine I could almost detect the whiff of a cigar. The drapes at the window are a deep red grass, the valence softened by golden yellow yarrow blossoms (Achillea millefolium). The rug on the floor matches, though the yellow bands are from soft conga grass (Bracharia ruziziensis).

A grandfather clock in the corner is made from a gnarled piece of wood. The face is a piece of papyrus, the numbers are marked with red yarrow petals.

It took me a while to decipher what the soft leather-like material was but finally concluded it is from magnolia petals, which stay soft and supple even as they turn a rich brown. Both the boots and satchel are made from this.

1 1/2"

Magnolia grandiflora

The magnolia petals were stitched with yucca fibers to make the satchel.

Cards on the table seem to be made from pressed dogwood petals. Raspberry juice hearts and diamonds, pokeweed berry juice for clubs and spades. The table top is a smooth, mahogany-like magnolia leaf. Maybe they dried it under stones to keep it absolutely flat.

I peeked into the journal but the writing
is so tiny I could not read it – even with a
magnifying glass. Besides, the script is foreign,
the alphabet one I have never seen before.

Yarrow
(Achillea
millefolium)

The face of the grandfather
clock is papyrus, the numbers are
marked with red yarrow petals.

A wall hanging that looks like a painted animal hide is actually from the magnolia petal as well. Primitive drawings look almost like hieroglyphics.

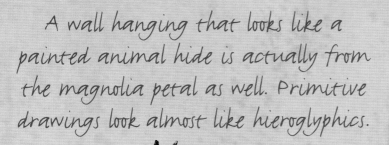

2 ¹/₂"

Lamb's ear
(stachys byzantina)

The warm coat is made from lamb's ear leaves (stachys byzantina) and is trimmed with brown magnolia petals which look, for all the world, like strips of leather.

111

Cue sticks are made of reeds, tips softened with fuzz from cattails. The handles are wrapped in different leaves.

Who ever guessed they would play pool! The table surface is a linden leaf, the balls are native berries — mostly holly.

Ball rack and holly balls.

Dear Katherine,

I have spent so much time exploring fairy houses that I have neglected my work. The Royal Horticultural Society has asked me to do an article on the native caladiums found on the island, so I set out today toward the interior of the island. When I saw an unusual orchid specimen in the underbrush and bent to examine it more closely, imagine how delighted I was to find it attached to a small bouquet — tied with raffia! The tiny bundle of flowers was so elegantly beautiful, it reminded me of a Japanese floral arrangement.

I crept deeper into the underbrush beside the river that intersects the island when all of a sudden I saw an amazing little red bridge spanning the tiniest rivulet of water. I could see faint footsteps in the

moss on either side of the bridge, which looked exactly like the bridges
I have seen in the gardens in Japan – only tiny in comparison. I peered
further down the path and found what I hoped to see – a tiny house
that looked as if it had grown right out of the rocks and moss.

Love, Grandmother

Caladium leaves
(Caladium bicolor)

the
Japanese
house

september 15

Back I went today to explore more fully. I first saw a small garden that had been intricately created. Raked sand and small stones were arranged so carefully, they looked as if they had been placed by an artist. Behind it stood the tiny house, obviously Japanese in style. I wonder if the fairies who built it are from Japan or simply love the serene lines of Japanese architecture. Some of the walls are paper made from mulberry leaves. The roof, too, is a thick paper, made with fibers of many different kinds of plants. It seems to have been treated with a waxy substance (beeswax?) to make it waterproof. Other walls are thin slices of wood.

2 3/4"

← The bright kite outside the door is made from the petals of a dahlia blossom. They must fly it, though it looks beautiful just as decoration in front of the door.

← The bouquet I found is made from a single, tiny oncidium orchid and a few blades of grass. Very simple. Very Oriental.

Dahlia (Dahlia x hybrid)

119

Rice stalk
(Oryza sativa)

Their shoes are outside the house, of course. Two pairs – the boots are made from rice stalks (Oryza sativa) and wrapped with tiny strands of red thread. The high sandals are made from cork wood (Quercus suber).

rice stalks

The garden in front of the house is typically Japanese — except for the size! A tiny stone lantern has ashes from wood chips in the base — I'm assuming they light it at night. The whole thing rests on a piece of small, dense moss.

6"

The garden looks so mani-cured, I'm sure they must clean the rocks and rake the sand daily. The rake seems to be made from slivers of miniature cat tail (Typha minima).

The red balsa wood bridge is a work of art. The rowboat is a sturdy little craft — made from okra pods. I never realized that they float. Koi fish (which look huge) swim gently toward the boat. I wonder if they could possibly help push the small boat through the water for the fairies?

The beauty of the inside took my breath away. It is characteristically Japanese - clean, elegant and simple. The floor is polished Asian birch wood (Betula platyphylla), the walls of thin paper. The back screen doors are made from skeletalized leaves. Just the veins remain, allowing plenty of light to filter through. A richly colored kimono hangs on the wall. It is all exquisitely done.

In the center of the room, on a woven mat, is a hibachi made from ebony wood, the center lined with copper, as they did it in the old days in Japan. The plates are pansy petals and the chopsticks appear to be no larger than single blades of dried grass.

pansy

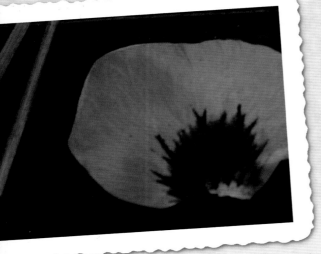

Ebony
(Diospyros ebenum)

A stone pot is full of rice — were the fairies just here? Were they eating? How did I miss them again!

There are four mats for sitting — looks like they are made from painted ginkgo leaves.

It looks as if Japanese maple leaves were hammered
on to papyrus and then hung on blue paper to make a scroll.
I can't be sure, of course, but I suspect that they dyed the paper
blue with indigo. I know it grows on the island.

Caladium leaves

bee balm

Bee balm plant
(Monarda didyma)

Next to the scroll hangs
a ceremonial kimono – made
from caladium leaves.

The top buttons are tiny rose
buds. The decoration along
each side is made from single
petals from the bee balm
plant (Monarda didyma).

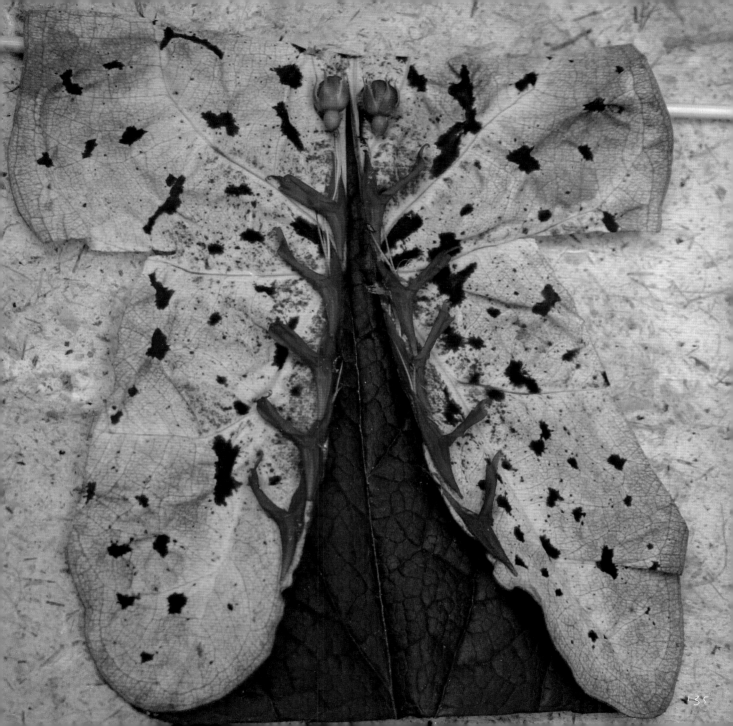

135

The fan on top of the chest is a painted ginkgo leaf (Ginkgo biloba).

The tea pot and cups are carved from gray stone.

Asian birch (Betula platyphylla)

The chest, too, is made of birch — with copper handles. The arrangement — bamboo vase and three slender blades of grass — is very simple and stylized, like most of their floral arrangements.

2"

The folding screen is made from pieces of ebony wood (Diospyos ebenum) and slim stems of wheat (Triticum aestivum). It is decorated with the chaff and seeds from the wheat plant. Each small piece of chaff looks like a tear drop, each tiny seed looks like a jewel. Who could imagine how beautiful that would be! The attention to detail is impressive. These fairies go far beyond function to make each piece a work of art.

Dear Katherine,

I am sitting in my own little house, watching the clouds gather over the mountains. I know that the rainy season is almost upon us. For the next few months, I'll stay close to home, drawing and writing and thinking about the fairy houses that I found.

What a magical spring and summer it was! My only regret was that I never actually saw a fairy. But even without seeing them, fairies brought an unexpected richness to my life. When I saw the first house, my whole idea of beauty changed. I began looking at things differently, examining a plant and

Wheat (Triticum aestivum)

wondering how a fairy would use it. A leaf suddenly became a pillow, a nutshell, a shoe. The more I saw, the more impressed I was with the beauty they found in the smallest of nature's creations. For example, I had never considered a kernel of wheat beautiful before, but on the Japanese screen, it became an object of exquisite loveliness. I suppose the greatest lesson from the fairies was a new way of seeing – of finding beauty in the tiniest detail.

It is my hope that as you look through these pages that you, too, will learn this lesson. Whether or not you "believe" in fairies or ever see one, remain open to their magic. Know that there is beauty everywhere, if you'll only take the time to look.

I love you,
Grandmother

glossary

Abelia *Abelia x grandiflora*
Abra clam *Divaricella quadrisulcata*
Acorn squash *Curcurbita maxima*
Almond *Prunus dulcis*
Amaranthus *Amaranthus caudatus*
Artichoke *Cynara scolymus*
Asian birch *Betula platyphylla*
Asparagus fern *Asparagus setaceus*
Asparagus *Asparagus officinalis*
Balsa wood *Ochroma lagopus*
Bamboo *Bambusa indigena*
Bay *Laurus nobilis*
Beans *Phaseolus vulgaris*
Bee balm *Monarda didyma*
Begonia *Begonia semperflorens*
Birch *Betula nigra*
Bittersweet *Celastrus scandens*
Black walnut *Juglans nigra*
Blueberry *Vaccinium ashei*
Brussels sprouts *Brassica oleracea var. gemmifera*
Caladium *Caladium bicolor*
Canteloupe *Cucumis melo*
Cattail *Typha latifolia*
Cedar cones *Cedrus deodora*
Cherry tomatoes *Lycopersican lycopersicum*
Cherry tree *Prunus serrotina*
Christmas fern *Polystichum acrostichoides*
Chrysanthemum *Chrysanthemum morifolum*
Cinnamon *Cinnamomum zeylanicum*
Cockscomb *Celosia cristata*
Coleus *Coleus blumei*
Conga grass *Bracharia ruzijiensis*
Cork wood *Quercus suber*
Corn *Zea mays rugosa*
Curly willow *Salix matsudana*
Dahlia *Dahlia x hybrid*
Dianthus *Dianthus*
Dogwood *Cornus florida*
Eastern white pine *Pinus strobus*
Ebony *Diospyros ebenum*
Euonymus *Euonymus fortunei*
Fairy tern *Cygis alba rothschildi*
False aster *Astermoea mongolica*
Flowering kale *Brassica oleraceae var. acephala*
Foxglove *Digitalis purpurea*
Ginger *Zingiber officinale*

Ginkgo *Ginkgo biloba*
Globe amaranth *Gomphrena globosa*
Gourd *Curcurbita*
Grass *Calamagrostis acutifolia*
Grass, black *Cortaderia*
Grass, yellow *Cortaderia sellonana*
Hibiscus *Hibiscus rosa-sinensis*
Hickory *Carya cordiformis*
Holly *Ilex cornuta*
Hosta *Hosta plantaginea*
Impatiens *Impatiens wallerana*
Indigo *Indigo fera*
Japanese maple *Acer japonicum*
Kiwi *Actinidia deliciosa*
Lady peas *Pisum sativum*
Lamb's ear *Stachys byzantina*
Larkspur *Consolida ambigua*
Lavender *Lavendula angustifolia*
Lenten rose *Helleborus niger*
Lichen (fan shaped) *Melanelia fuliginosa*
Lichen *Coriolus versicolor*
Lichen *Daedela contragosa*
Lichen, blue green *Ramalina stenospora*
Linden tree *Tilia euchlora*
Lobelia *Lobelia erinus*
Lurid dwarf triton *Ocenebra poulsoni*
Magnolia *Magnolia grandiflora*
Mica *Biotite mineral*
Miniature cattail *Typha minima*
Mini-rose *Rosa 'Baby Darling'*
Monkey puzzle *Araucaria*
Moss, green *Thidium delicatulum*
Mulberry *Morus nigra*
Mushrooms *Agaricus campestris*
Mustard *Brassica oleracea*
Okra *Abelmoschus esculentus*
Orchid *Dendrobium*
Palm *Phoenix canariensis*
Palm, coconut *Cocos nucifera*
Pansy *Viola wittrockiana*
Paper birch *Betula papyrifera*
Papyrus *Cyperus papyrus*
Peanut *Vigna unguiculata*
Pearl onions *Allium cepa*
Pecan *Carya illinoiensis*
Pentas *Pentas lanceolata*

Peppercorn *Piper nigrum*
Peppers *Capsicum annuum*
Persian violet *Exacum affine*
Persimmon *Diospyros virginiana*
Phlox *Phlox divericata*
Pine *Pinus echinata*
Pistachio *Pistacia chinensis*
Pokeberry *Phytolacca americana*
Poplar tree *Populus alba*
Purple pitcher plant *Sarracenia purpurea*
Poppy *Papaver rhoeas*
Quail egg *Callipepla californicus*
Quince *Chaenomeles quinoa*
Radishes *Raphanus sativus*
Raffia *Raphia ruffia*
Raspberry *Rhus idaeus*
Rattlesnake plantain *Goodyera pubescens*
Red abalone *Haliotis rufescens*
Red grass *Pennisetum alopecuroides*
Rice *Oryza sativa*
Rockcress *Arabis alpina*
Rose *Rosa*
Rosemary *Rosemarinus*
Sage *Salvia officinalis*
Sand bur *Cenchrus pauciflorus*
Sand dollar *Echinarachnius parma*
Scallop, bay *Argopecten irradians*
Sea heather *Erica carnea*
Sea horse *Hippocampus erectus*
Sensitive plant *Schrankia microphylla*
Spanish moss *Tillandsia usneoides*
Speedwell *Veronica prostrata*
Star anise *Illicium vernum*
Star fruit *Averrhoa carambola*
Statice *Limonium latifolium*
Thistle *Cirsium vulgare.*
Tulip poplar *Liriodendron tulipifera*
Turkey tail fungus *Trametes versicolor*
Turnip *Brassica rapa*
Veronica *Veronica prostrata*
Viola *Viola cornuta*
Wall flower *Erysimum cheiri*
Walnut *Juglans cinera*
Wheat *Triticum aestivum*
Yarrow *Achillea millefolium*
Yucca *Hesperaloe parviflora*

Fairy Island

Northern Forest

Farm House

← fairy path

river →

West Mountains

Garden Villa

bridge

Japanese House

3 miles